BIG HEAD no. 7,444,635,142

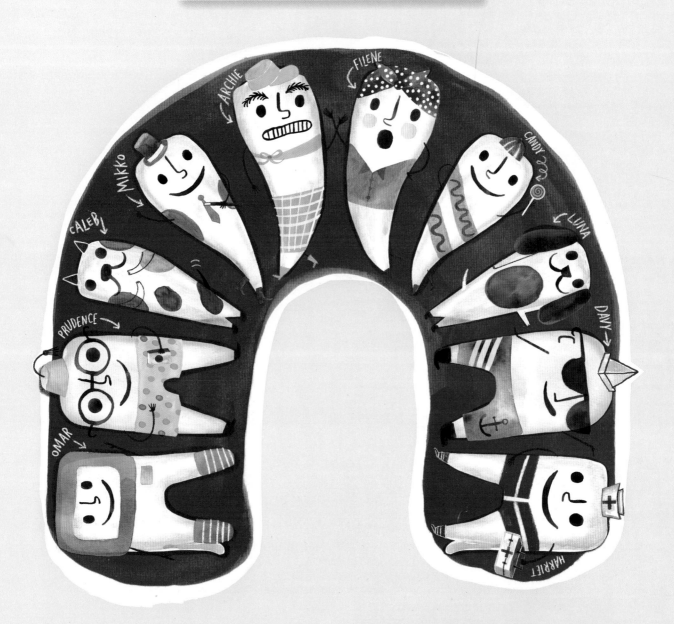

Lower Mouth

For my husband, Jeremy, and two
children, Rooksby and Hugo

— T.C.B.

All rights reserved. Published in the United States by Random House Children's Books,
a division of Penguin Random House LLC, New York.

Random House and the colophon are registered trademarks of Penguin Random House LLC.

Visit us on the Web! rhcbooks.com

Educators and librarians, for a variety of teaching tools,
visit us at RHTeachersLibrarians.com

Library of Congress Cataloging-in-Publication Data
Name: Burke, Tyler Clark, author, illustrator.
Title: The last loose tooth / Tyler Clark Burke.
Description: First edition. | New York : Random House Children's Books, [2020] | Audience: Ages 3–7. |
Audience: Grades K–1. | Summary: "Lou is the last loose baby tooth, and he's just not ready to make the leap
and leave the mouth . . . until all the other baby teeth are gone and Lou must face his fear." —Provided by publisher.
Identifiers: LCCN 2019036149 (print) | LCCN 2019036150 (ebook) | ISBN 978-0-593-12144-3 (hardcover) |
ISBN 978-0-593-12145-0 (library binding) | ISBN 978-0-593-12146-7 (ebook)
Subjects: CYAC: Teeth—Fiction. | Fear—Fiction.
Classification: LCC PZ7.1.B878 Las 2020 (print) | LCC PZ7.1.B878 (ebook) | DDC [E]—dc23

MANUFACTURED IN CHINA

10 9 8 7 6 5 4 3 2 1

First Edition

THE LAST LOOSE TOOTH

Hi there! I'm Lou!

Tyler Clark Burke

Random House  New York

It was a perfectly ordinary night....

Until it wasn't.

Arlene and Margo were the
first teeth to make the leap.
They lived at the top front of
the mouth and loved attention.

The lower teeth started chattering.

The upper teeth, where I lived, went quiet. Quiet except for a loudmouth named Cary.

Cary didn't realize his days in the mouth were numbered. Rotten to the core, he was yanked from the mouth three days after Halloween.

Filene and Archie, the oldest and crankiest teeth, mumbled their disapproval.

The rest of us continued chewing, chomping, and biting,
completely unaware we were SLOWLY being pushed out.
The mouth was the only home we'd ever known.

Davy came loose in the
bath and surfed straight
down the drain.

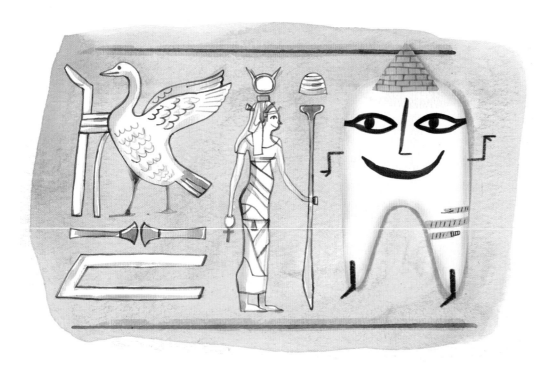

Farrow tumbled out of the mouth and
into her favorite museum exhibit.

Omar was tied to a rocket with a piece of floss, and . . .

5 · 4 · 3 · 2 · 1

. . . AWAY HE WENT!

After that, some of the teeth started really freaking out.

I won't say who.

But it wasn't just me! I swear.
Some of the looser teeth were also upset.

Excuse me! Hello! Order in the mouth!
The rumors are true. We MUST depart.
CRIKEY!

Clever Harriet knew just what to say.

Once I calmed down, Harriet decided to make her exit. She hopped out of the mouth, skittered across the counter, and climbed atop her favorite toy.

Three of the canines—Wolfy, Luna, and Caleb—
each left on a different harvest moon.

Patch hopped down the plank of a
toothpick before diving into the deep.

Mikko vanished in smoke.

Wylie slipped into a banana.

Esmé ghosted in Paris.

It went on like this for years, teeth leaving left and right, up and down, until the only one left . . . was me.

I felt really alone. . . .

Even though I was surrounded by adults.

BORING adults.

Whenever I asked the big teeth to give me a hand, they said they were too busy.

I was STUCK.

Until . . .

ONE MORNING . . .

I felt a little bit different.

With an extra wiggle, and an extra jiggle,
I CAME OUT!

I was carried upstairs to a big white pillow.

I was placed in a little box that opened just like a mouth.

And closed just like a mouth!

It was the Tooth Fairy! *My* Tooth Fairy!

She came to take me to the Great Land of Teeth!

And even though I tried
to protest . . .

But I'm not ready!
I need toothpaste!
I need floss!

You are
ready, Lou!

. . . she promised to take care of me.

We're off to the GREAT LAND of TEETH! Say goodbye to the clouds down beneath. To vanish we must!

Twirl in FAIRY DUST! Pip PIP! TALLY-HO! Tiddle Dee!
Are we there yet?
We are!

TOOTH FAMILY DIAGRAM

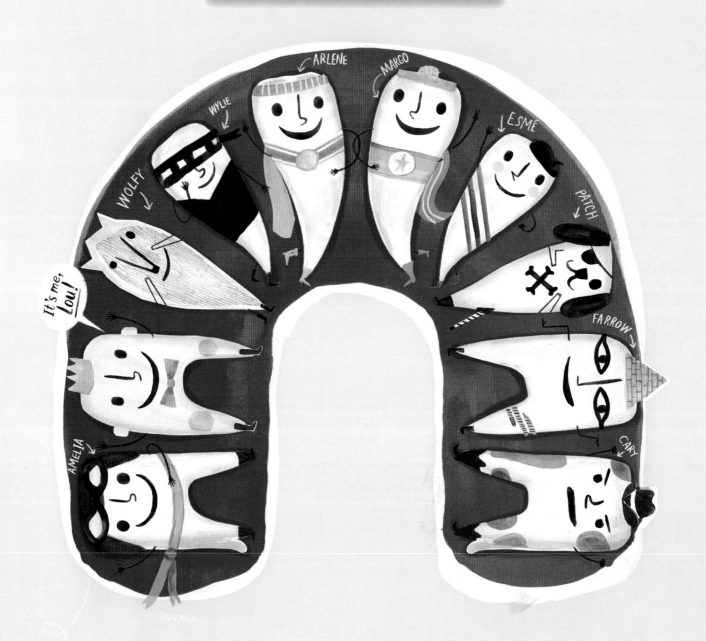

Upper Mouth